WHAT A TEAM!

By Calliope Glass
Illustrated by the Disney Storybook Art Team

A Random House PICTUREBACK® Book
Random House 🏠 New York

randomhousekids.com
ISBN 978-0-7364-3688-5
Printed in the United States of America
10 9 8 7 6 5 4 3 2

It was winter in Arendelle—and the happiest winter in many years.

Princess Anna and Kristoff were reading in the castle when they heard the sound of children's laughter outside. Anna went to the window to see what was going on.

"Oh!" she said. "Come look, Kristoff. It's so cute!"

REINDEER VENTRILOQUISM FOR FUN AND PROFIT

Kristoff and Anna saw three children building a toboggan in the snowy courtyard below. Kristoff smiled at the scene, but Anna could tell he was thinking about something else.

"Out with it," she said. "What's on your mind?"

Kristoff turned to Anna. "Every year, ice harvesters from all over the world, and their friends and family, gather for the Ice Games," he said. "I bet those kids are getting ready for the toboggan race. I've always wanted to compete in the Games. I'd like to sign up this year, but I don't know where I'd find teammates."

Later, Anna told Elsa what Kristoff had said.

"There aren't any royal events going on this weekend," said Anna, "so I was thinking—"

"—that we should offer to be Kristoff's teammates!" Elsa finished, delighted.

Anna hugged her sister. "This will be so much fun!"

Anna and Elsa rushed to tell Kristoff about their plan.

"You guys are the best!" Kristoff said. "Now, some of the events can be pretty challenging. And, Elsa, you can't use your magic powers."

"Of course not," Elsa agreed. "We'll make a great team—no magic needed!"

The next day, the friends arrived at the Ice Games. It was the first day of the competition, and they got in line to sign up for the events.

"Say, isn't that the Queen of Arendelle?" said an ice harvester, pointing at Elsa.

"Hello, everyone!" Elsa said to the crowd. "Who's excited to compete?"

A group from Arendelle—
including the children Anna and
Kristoff had seen from the palace
window—cheered the loudest. They
were proud to have a queen who
liked to have fun!

Anna grinned. She loved that the
people of Arendelle were so fond of
her sister.

The first event was ice sculpting.

"Competitors have two hours to sculpt whatever they choose," said the announcer. "Be creative, and have fun!"

With just a hammer and a chisel—no magic—Elsa carved a gorgeous ice sculpture of the rock trolls. She won first place!

Next, Anna and Kristoff were ready to compete.

"I don't care what the event is," said Anna. "I know we're going to win!"

"Time for couples ice-skating!" said the announcer.

"Unless it's that," Anna said as her heart sank. She thought she was a terrible ice-skater.

But the princess wasn't one to back down from a challenge. She and Kristoff did their best, speeding around the rink. Kristoff managed a little jump, and Anna only fell nine times. They didn't win, but they had a lot of fun trying . . . and they came in third!

That night at dinner, Anna, Elsa, and Kristoff discussed the competition.

"With Elsa's first-place finish, and Kristoff and me coming in third, we actually stand a chance of winning the Ice Games!" Anna said.

Kristoff agreed. "All we need to do is win the toboggan race tomorrow," he said.

"Good luck," said a small voice.

Anna turned to see the little girl from Arendelle.

"Thank you," Anna replied with a smile. "You made the ice sculpture of the palace today, right?"

The girl nodded.

"It was beautiful," Elsa said. "And I know a little something about making ice palaces!"

The girl giggled and ran back to sit with her family.

"Good luck to you, too!" Anna called.

"What a sweet girl," Elsa said. "She reminds me of someone else at her age."

"Me?" Anna asked hopefully.

"Of course I meant you," Elsa said, smiling. "I wish I had been able to do more fun things with you when we were young."

"Well, we're making up for that now," Anna said. "I'm having a blast!"

"It will be an even bigger blast if we win tomorrow," Kristoff said. "Let's finish our hot chocolate and get a good night's sleep."

Early the next morning, Anna, Elsa, and Kristoff
piled onto their toboggan at the top of a steep hill.
It was time for the last event of the Ice Games.

"Here we gooooooo!" Anna shrieked. The trio
rocketed down the slope with the rest of the racers.

Their toboggan went faster and faster, and they
quickly pulled ahead of the other teams.

"We're winning!" Anna cried.

Suddenly another toboggan streaked down the slope and crossed the finish line first. The winners were the children from Arendelle!

"We won! We won!" the kids shouted happily, hugging each other and jumping up and down.

Watching them celebrate, Anna didn't feel disappointed that her team hadn't won. She just hoped Kristoff wasn't upset.

"I'm sorry we didn't win first place, Kristoff," Elsa said later, when they stood together on the winners' podium.

Kristoff grinned. "Don't be. I finally got to compete in the Ice Games! And I think it's great that they won. Having friends you can count on is really important when you're a kid."

Anna hugged Kristoff. "Having friends
you can count on is really important *forever*.
And I have the best friends of all!"